IMAGINE THAT

Licensed exclusively to Imagine That Publishing Ltd
Tide Mill Way, Woodbridge, Suffolk, IP12 1AP, UK
www.imaginethat.com
Copyright © 2019 Imagine That Group Ltd
All rights reserved
0 2 4 6 8 9 7 5 3 1
Manufactured in China

Retold by Joshua George
Illustrated by Dania Florino

ISBN 978-1-78700-902-8

A catalogue record for this book is available from the British Library

The Wizard of Oz

Illustrated by Dania Florino
Retold by Joshua George

Dorothy lived on a farm in Kansas with her aunt and uncle and her little dog, Toto. One morning, Dorothy heard a strange whooshing noise outside the house – a whirlwind was coming! Before Dorothy could hide, the window blew open and something hit her on the head.

As she fell to the floor, she felt the house rise in the air and start to spin ...

around and around and around and around!

When Dorothy woke up, the wind had stopped and the house was still. Cautiously, she opened the door.

'Goodness!' she exclaimed.
'This doesn't look like Kansas!'

Then Dorothy spotted a crowd of people.

'Thank you for saving us from the Wicked Witch of the East!'

cried the crowd, happily.

And there, sticking out from under the house, were two feet wearing red shoes.

Dorothy had landed on the Witch!

'Don't worry, dear,' said a tall lady. 'You're in the land of Oz, and I'm Glinda, the Good Witch.'

'But how do I get home to Kansas?' asked Dorothy.

'The Wizard of Oz can help,' replied Glinda. 'Take the Wicked Witch of the East's magic shoes and follow the yellow brick road to the Emerald City. You'll find him there.'

Nearby, the Wicked Witch of the West was hiding. She was angry because Dorothy had landed on her sister and was even wearing her magic shoes!

'I want those shoes,' she hissed.

Dorothy and Toto set off along the yellow brick road. As they passed a field, Dorothy was amazed to see a Scarecrow wink and wave at her!

Dorothy stopped and chatted to the Scarecrow, telling him all about her journey to the Emerald City.

'Maybe the Wizard could give me some brains!' said the Scarecrow hopefully.

'Then why don't you come too?'
asked Dorothy, and they set off together.

oon, Dorothy, Toto and the Scarecrow met a man made of tin, who squeaked with every step.

'I'll help you oil those creaky joints,' Dorothy said, kindly, telling him about their journey as she did so.

'Perhaps the Wizard could give me a heart,' said the Tin Man, hopefully.

Later that day, a Lion bounded out of the woods and Toto barked at him, bravely.

'Boo hoo,' cried the Lion. 'I'm supposed to be King of the Animals, but I don't have any courage.'

'Come with us to see the Wizard,' suggested Dorothy, so he did!

After a very long walk, the friends spotted the green glow of the Emerald City.

'Look!' exclaimed Dorothy as they got closer. 'Everything is green ... even the people!'

The friends went to see the Wizard straight away.

'I'll help you all if you bring me the Wicked Witch
of the West's broomstick,' he said.

'We'll have to do it,' said the Lion, 'or I'll never get my courage.'
'Or my brains!' said the Scarecrow.
'Or my heart!' said the Tin Man.

'And I'll never get back to Kansas!' cried Dorothy.

So the friends set off towards the Wicked Witch's castle in the West.

They crossed mountains full of lurking wolves ...

and tiptoed through forests full of scary bees and glowing eyes!

But the Wicked Witch found out that they were coming and sent a troop of flying monkeys to stop them!

The Lion roared! The Tin Man swung his axe!
And even the Scarecrow tried to fight!
But the monkeys grabbed Dorothy and Toto and
dragged them to the Wicked Witch's castle.

'Ha-ha-HA!' cackled the Wicked Witch. 'Now the magic shoes are mine!'

The Wicked Witch was so excited about the shoes that she didn't notice Toto creep away to find the others to help Dorothy escape. Soon, the friends had sneaked into the castle and freed Dorothy.

When the Witch saw what was happening,
she shot sparks at the Scarecrow who burst into flames!

Quickly, Dorothy threw a bucket
of water over her friend.

'Eeek!'

she squealed in surprise,
as some water splashed the
Wicked Witch and turned
her into a giant puddle!

Dorothy grabbed the Wicked Witch's broomstick and the friends headed back to the Emerald City. 'Now the Wizard will have to help us!' she said. But they were in for a surprise!

'I'm afraid I can't help you,' said the Wizard. 'I'm just a normal man. I floated here in a hot-air balloon and everyone thought I was a wizard!'

Dorothy started to cry, and so did the Scarecrow,
the Tin Man and the Lion.

'But I can give you these,' said the Wizard,
handing the Scarecrow a certificate,
the Tin Man a clockwork heart and
the Lion a big medal for bravery.

TOP
BRAVERY

'What about me?' said Dorothy, sadly.

'Don't worry,' said the Wizard.
'I'll take you home in my hot-air balloon!'

But just as they were about to take off,
Toto jumped out of the basket and ran off!

'Wait!' yelled Dorothy,
leaping out after him.

'I'm sorry,' said the Wizard, as the balloon

floated away. 'I can't stop it!'

Dorothy started to cry.

'How will I ever get home?' she sobbed.

Then, with a puff of smoke and a shower of rainbow-coloured sparkles, another witch appeared.

'Don't cry,' she said. 'I'm the Good Witch of the South.
You've helped your friends, so I'm going to help YOU!
Just click your heels together three times, say,
"There's no place like home,"
and you'll see!'

So Dorothy said goodbye to her friends.

'I'll miss you all so much,' she said. Then, holding Toto tightly, she clicked her heels three times and said,

'There's no place like home.'

Suddenly, she was back in Kansas!
There was her house – and her aunt and uncle.

'What an adventure!' she thought.
'But the Good Witch of the South was right.
There really is no place like home!'

Join Dorothy on her magical adventure in the land of Oz in this adaptation of L. Frank Baum's timeless classic.

Illustrated by Dania Florino
Retold by Joshua George

IMAGINE THAT™

Licensed exclusively to Imagine That Publishing Ltd
Tide Mill Way, Woodbridge, Suffolk, IP12 1AP, UK
www.imaginethat.com
Copyright © 2019 Imagine That Group Ltd
All rights reserved
0246897531
Manufactured in China

RRP £6.99
ISBN 978-1-78700-902-8

9 781787 009028

KT-908-801

TMP-PCF-32-1908-167